Pooh's
Scavenger
Hunt

Disney's
Winnie the Pooh First Readers

Disney's
A Winnie the Pooh First Reader

Pooh's Scavenger Hunt

by Isabel Gaines
ILLUSTRATED BY Studio Orlando

DISNEY PRESS

NEW YORK

First Edition

1 3 5 7 9 10 8 6 4 2

Library of Congress Catalog Card Number: 98-89816

ISBN: 0-7868-4317-9 (paperback)

For more Disney Press fun, visit www.DisneyBooks.com

Pooh's Scavenger Hunt

It was a sunny day
in the Hundred-Acre Wood.
Christopher Robin was sitting
on a tree stump when Pooh
and all his friends
came to say hello.

"Hello, Christopher Robin," said Pooh.

"What are we going to do today?"

"Why don't we have

a scavenger hunt?"

said Christopher Robin.

"Tiggers love scavenger hunts!"

yelled Tigger.

"What is a scavenger hunt?"

"A scavenger hunt is a game
where you hunt for things,"
said Christopher Robin.

"What kinds of things?" asked Rabbit.

Christopher Robin scratched his head.

"Oh, let me think."

"Why don't you look for

a purple flower,

a small jar of honey,

and a red leaf?"

Christopher Robin smiled.

"And then,

I want you to find

the greatest thing

in the whole world."

13

Pooh was confused.

"Isn't honey the greatest thing

in the whole world?"

he asked.

"Honey is grcat,"

said Christopher Robin.

"But there is something

even greater."

So Pooh and his friends

went into the forest to search.

They went to Pooh's house first,

for that was the best place

to find honey.

"Up there is my only
small jar of honey,"
said Pooh.
"How will we
get it down?"

"Climb on my shoulders,"

said Tigger.

"I still can't reach it," said Pooh.

"Rabbit, can you help?"

19

"I can't quite reach.

Maybe if Roo helped, too?"

said Rabbit.

Roo grabbed the jar of honey,

and dropped it to Kanga.

Kanga put it in a bag.

"Next we need a leaf
and a flower," said Pooh.
"Does anybody remember
which should be red
and which should be purple?"
No one did.

"Well," said Pooh.

"Here is a red flower.

And it smells nice."

"Then it's perfect," said Kanga.

Everyone agreed.

"I found a leaf,"

Roo called.

"But it is not purple."

"I have some purple paint
at my house," said Rabbit.
"We can paint the leaf purple."
And that's what they did.

"Now all we need
is the greatest thing
in the whole world,"
said Piglet.

They headed back

into the woods.

"Greatest thing," called Pooh,

"where are you?"

They walked and walked.

Soon, it grew quite late—

and quite dark.

They all held hands

so no one would get lost.

Finally they found

Christopher Robin,

sitting on the tree stump.

They were back

where they had started.

"Hello," said
Christopher Robin.
"Are you done with
the scavenger hunt?"

"No," said Pooh sadly.

"We all searched together."

"And found everything," said Tigger.

"Except for the greatest thing

in the whole world,"

said Rabbit.

Christopher Robin smiled.

"But you did!

You found the greatest thing

in the whole world."

"We did?" they all asked.

"Oh, yes.

You searched together,"

said Christopher Robin.

"Friends working together
is the greatest thing
in the whole world.
I knew you would find it!"

Can you match the words with the pictures?

leaf

jar

Pooh

Christopher Robin

tree stump

36

Fill in the missing letters.

re_

cl_mb

flo_er

Rabbi_

_ag